Trivia Queen, 3rd Grade Supreme

by **Derrick Barnes**

illustrated by **Vanessa Brantley Newton**

SCHOLASTIC INC.

New York   Toronto   London   Auckland   Sydney
Mexico City   New Delhi   Hong Kong   Buenos Aires

The author would like to give special thanks
to Andrea Pinkney and Regina Brooks.

No part of this publication may be reproduced, stored
in a retrieval system, or transmitted in any form or by any means,
electronic, mechanical, photocopying, recording, or otherwise, without
written permission of the publisher. For information regarding permission,
write to Scholastic Inc., Attention: Permissions Department, 557 Broadway,
New York, NY 10012.

ISBN-13: 978-0-545-01761-9   ISBN-10: 0-545-01761-0

Text copyright © 2008 by Derrick Barnes
Illustrations copyright © 2008 by Scholastic Inc.

All rights reserved. Published by Scholastic Inc.

SCHOLASTIC, LITTLE APPLE, and associated logos are trademarks
and/or registered trademarks of Scholastic Inc.

Library of Congress Cataloging-in-Publication Data Available

12 11 10 9 8   15 16 17 18 19/0

Printed in the U.S.A.   40
First printing, July 2008

To E. Solo, and the Chocolate Boy Thunder –
my very own Booker Boys
(sorry, no Ruby . . . yet)

⭐ Chapters ⭐

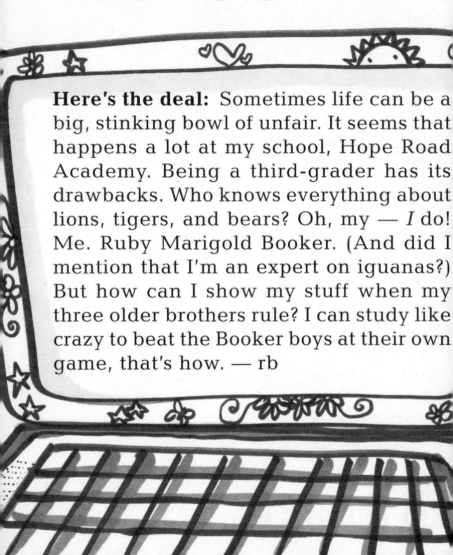

⋆ Ruby's Laptop Journal ⋆

Here's the deal: Sometimes life can be a big, stinking bowl of unfair. It seems that happens a lot at my school, Hope Road Academy. Being a third-grader has its drawbacks. Who knows everything about lions, tigers, and bears? Oh, my — *I* do! Me. Ruby Marigold Booker. (And did I mention that I'm an expert on iguanas?) But how can I show my stuff when my three older brothers rule? I can study like crazy to beat the Booker boys at their own game, that's how. — rb

Dodge This!

It was down to me and only me.

We were playing ball tag in gym class against Mr. Littlejohn's third-grade class. Ball tag is freeze tag and dodgeball put together. Kids from our classroom, Pluto-3, were on one side of the bright white line on the gym floor. Mr. Littlejohn's class was on the other side. There were two boys on their side against me. The other kids from my class were frozen solid.

Lenny Sermon and Mikey Tripp,

the boys from the other class, passed the ball back and forth between them. Mikey yelled out, "Just stand still, Ruby. Let's get this over with." And then Lenny had to add his three cents. "You don't stand a chance, girl." He laughed.

Even though my classmates were stuck like statues, they were all cheering me on. Low-Low, who speaks quiet as a mouse, waved both of his arms in the air. "Come on, Ruby. You're our last hope," he said. Normally, Low-Low talks so quietly I can't hear a thing he says. That's how he got the name Low-Low.

But today Low-Low was calling out like a cheerleader! I've never heard him be so loud. Maybe this was because our team had lost ball tag last week for the second time in a row, all from Low-Low's lousy playing. After that game everybody in our class blamed Low-Low for making Pluto-3 into such losers. I knew then that I had to win for Low-Low and represent my class.

All of a sudden, I shouted, "PLUTO-3!!!" My classmates screamed along with me, "PLUTO-3!" I was ready then. "Throw the ball!" I said as I rubbed my palms together.

My brother Roosevelt, who we call Ro, taught me how to stand when you're waiting for a ball to come flying at you — feet spread wide, hands open and ready to catch the ball. So, that's just what I did. Just like Ro had showed me.

Lenny passed the ball to Mikey. He stepped back and waited for our gym teacher, Coach Tuma, to blow his whistle. Everybody in the gym got quiet.

Mikey rushed the bright white line like he was a wild rhino. I stood there and waited for the perfect moment. When the ball flew out of Mikey's hands, I could hear Lenny cheering like they had already won. I'd played dozens of dodgeball games with my three brothers, and the ball that Mikey threw at me seemed kind of weak. It almost looked like slow motion.

I reached out and plucked the ball out of the air like it was a cherry. Mikey's jaw hit the gym floor. He couldn't believe it, but he was out.

Lenny knew he was next. He stopped laughing and looked like a scared little chicken. He tried to turn and run for the wall, but *I* charged the white line this time.

Lenny fell as he tried to escape and then got back on his feet. Before he could take two steps, I chucked the ball like I had a cannon for an arm. Lenny turned back and saw that ball zooming toward him. He hollered, "Nooooooo!" But it was too late. The ball bounced off the heel of Lenny's sneaker and then *bonked!* him in the back of the head. I didn't mean for the ball to hit Lenny that way. He hit the floor before he could reach the wall. Game over.

Who else could have defeated those boys while wearing the cutest pink-and-gold skirt with brand-new purple and orange mismatched sneakers? Ruby Marigold Booker, that's who. I couldn't help but sing:

"Ball tag champions, can't you see,
Ruby Booker and the class from
Pluto-3!"

I raised my hands like a champion. My frozen teammates came back to life. Teresa Petticoat, my best friend in the universe, cheered at the top of her lungs, "HOORAY FOR RUBY!!!!" I'd won the game for my whole class. Low-Low gave me the highest high five ever. Winning was for Low-Low and everyone in Pluto-3. That was good news.

But right after ball tag ended, our gym teacher, Coach Tuma, had even better news.

"Great job, Ruby!" Coach Tuma smiled at me. He gave me a high five. He had a very proper way of talking, though. "Your classroom should be ever so grateful to you,"

he said. Coach Tuma was from an African country called Kenya. I liked his voice.

"Thank you, Coach Tuma," I said.

"You ran at those boys with so much power and speed," Coach Tuma said. He pointed at the painting on the wall of the gym. "You see the African elephant in that beautiful painting, Ruby? You have the same grace."

Teresa was right by my side. "Yeah," she agreed. "Ruby is all grace," she said.

I tapped Coach Tuma on his arm. "Coach, I don't mean to be rude, but that's *not* an African elephant."

Coach Tuma looked up at the painting again. "What do you mean?" He crossed his arms.

"It's simple, Coach Tuma," I explained. "That elephant has small ears, and his back has a little dent in it.

That, Coach Tuma, is an *Asian* elephant."

"You're sure about that?" he asked. Coach Tuma was smiling. I could tell he knew I was right, but he just wanted to test me.

Teresa said, "She's positive, Coach Tuma. Trust me, Ruby knows what she's talking about."

I bumped my hip to Teresa's. "I do know, Coach. I just saw that elephant on one of the animal facts Web sites my ma lets me go to."

"So, Ruby, you're an animal expert?"

"Nope. I'm a *trivia* expert. When it comes to little facts, strange facts, and funny facts about any- and everything, there's a good chance I know it."

"There's a *great* chance she knows it," Teresa said.

"Well, it's a good thing you know so much about animals," Coach Tuma said. "My wife is here at school today. She is the head zookeeper at the Bellow Rock City Zoo. She'll be bringing a surprise to every classroom. Who knows? Maybe it's animals."

"*Really?!* I love animals. I have a pet iguana named Lady Love," I said. But Teresa wasn't so happy. She's scared of anything that crawls, slithers, barks, chirps, or squeaks. I have to lock up my pet iguana when she comes to my house. I put my arm around Teresa. "Will your wife be bringing iguanas?" I asked Coach Tuma.

"She'll be bringing many interesting things, Ruby, including a big announcement," Coach Tuma said. "But you'll just have to wait and see."

"What announcement?" I wanted to know.

Teresa backed away. "Does the announcement have anything to do with *touching* the animals?"

"She'll be in your classroom next. Soon you'll know exactly what's coming," Coach Tuma said.

I hate it when people keep secrets.

But Coach Tuma wouldn't tell us anything else. He blew his whistle for the class to line up.

I was still excited about winning at ball tag, but now my mind was stuck on the big announcement. What could it be?

2
Animal Expert

"**S**ounds like we have a visitor," our teacher, Miss Fuqua, announced after hearing a tiny knock on our classroom door. Teresa jumped out of her seat like it was on fire. She ran under Miss Fuqua's desk and peeked out at our teacher.

"Now, Miss Fuqua," she said, "those creepy, itchy, biting, scratchy, slimy critters and I just don't get along." Teresa looked as scared as ever.

"You can stay right where you are, Teresa. I don't mind," Miss Fuqua said.

A second knock came from the door, and in walked a lady wearing a cute tan outfit. Behind her was a tall man pulling two covered cages behind him. Miss Fuqua asked us to sit around the big earth-patterned rug in our classroom. "Keep your legs crossed and your hands in your laps," she instructed. But I didn't want to put my hands in my lap. I wanted to pet the animals!

The lady in the tan outfit introduced herself. "Hello, students of Pluto-3. I am the head zookeeper at the Bellow Rock City Zoo." She had the same proper way of talking as Coach Tuma. "My name is —" Before she could finish, I stood up and waved my hands in the air.

"I know who you are. You're Coach Tuma's wife. And I know that you're from Kenya because you talk the same way he does. And —" Now Miss Fuqua cut me off.

"Ruby Booker! You're a smart girl, so I know you haven't lost your manners or your mind. We don't interrupt guests, do we, class?" Miss Fuqua asked. Together, everyone said, "Noooooo!"

Sometimes, I just can't help myself. I didn't mean to be rude. But I hate waiting on stuff. Especially when it's right in front of me. I was dying to see what was under those cage covers. Were they lizards, or badgers, or bear cubs? I rocked back and forth, cracking my knuckles and tapping my toes on the floor.

The zoo lady had her eyes on me. "Yes, I am the coach's wife," she said. "My name is Mrs. Teema Tuma. Animals are my job." She didn't seem too upset by my blurting out. I was glad about that.

She turned to the man behind her. "This is my assistant today, boys and girls. His name is Earl." The man named Earl didn't say much. He

waved once. In a deep voice he said, "Hello, everybody. Glad to be here." Even though Earl didn't have much to say, I was going to be really nice to him so that he and Mrs. Tuma would let me pet the animals. No more blurting out. I wanted to be treated special.

Earl gently pulled the covers off the cages. "Those are the cutest little monkeys," Low-Low said quietly.

But I knew they weren't. I couldn't help but do what I was trying so hard not to do! "Those are baby orangutans!" Mrs. Tuma looked pleased that I knew what was in the cages. She held one of the orangutans. Earl held the other one. They walked around our circle to let us get a closer look.

Teresa was so far underneath Miss Fuqua's desk, I couldn't even see her anymore.

"These lovely creatures are from Asia, boys and girls," Mrs. Tuma said. But the way they drank milk from their baby bottles and looked at us with their big soupy eyes, it looked like they came from a little bitty country called Cute.

When Mrs. Tuma and Earl put the orangutans away and locked

the cages, Teresa Petticoat joined us around the rug.

"Students, listen up. Mrs. Tuma has a *big, big, big* announcement to share," Miss Fuqua said.

When the room got completely quiet, Mrs. Tuma said, "Next week, here at Hope Road Academy, I will be back for the annual schoolwide animal trivia contest that will be held in your beautiful auditorium."

I heard everything she said, but the word that came through the loudest was my favorite word — *trivia*! Trivia was my thing. I wanted to blurt out again, but I kept listening. *Contest* was another one of my favorite words. And the two together were beautiful. *Trivia contest.*

Mrs. Tuma explained. "The student who answers all of the trivia questions correctly will win free passes to the Bellow Rock City Zoo for the whole year . . . for every student in his or her grade level." When Mrs. Tuma said that, everyone in our class went crazy. The hoots and hollers got even louder when she added, "Plus . . . the whole thing will be seen on a local TV station!" But everyone groaned when Mrs. Tuma finished her announcement. "The trivia contest will be for fifth- through eighth-graders. As third-graders, your job is to cheer on your fellow students."

We wasted all those hoots and hollers for nothing!

Now I just couldn't help it. I *had* to blurt out one more time. "That's not fair, Mrs. Tuma. Miss Fuqua, tell her, I'm really, really, really good at trivia!" I begged Miss Fuqua to back me up.

"I know it, Ruby, but rules are rules," Miss Fuqua said.

Mrs. Tuma said, "Young lady, don't worry. To be fair, we will provide take-home junior trivia booklets for kindergarten through fourth-grade students. Since the trivia questions are for older children, it would be unfair for students in the third grade and below to compete against seventh- and eighth-graders, don't you think?" Mrs. Tuma asked me.

"No way! I can beat those big ol' seventh- and eighth-graders any day. I can do it," I cried to Mrs. Tuma. "Besides, junior trivia booklets are for little kids who aren't that good at trivia. I'm as good as it gets."

"Well, it's fine with me if you want to enter the contest, but the final decision must come from your principal," Mrs. Tuma told me.

"Really?" I asked. I turned to Miss Fuqua and said, "Please, Miss Fuqua, I could win this thing. I know I could."

Miss Fuqua pulled Mrs. Tuma to the side and they began to talk. Slowly and quietly, my classmates began to chant. It was my girl Teresa who got the chanting started. *"Ruby! Ruby! Ruby!"*

The other kids wanted me to represent the third grade in the contest. They believed in me. They knew I could win those free zoo passes just like I won the ball tag game in the gym. I wore a smile that sparkled brighter than Miss Fuqua's earrings.

Miss Fuqua and Mrs. Tuma came back over to our circle. Miss Fuqua said, "Well, Ruby, it's okay with me and it's okay with Mrs. Tuma, so all we have to do is convince the principal, Ms. Cherrybaum." The class cheered. Miss Fuqua said, "Unfortunately, Ruby, Ms. Cherrybaum is out of town. She'll be back tomorrow. We'll ask her then."

Earl put the cloth covers back on the orangutan cages. As Mrs. Tuma waved good-bye and Earl rolled the cages out of our classroom, we all waved back. All I could think about was being on that big stage in our auditorium, looking

good on TV, and winning the whole
contest for the third grade. This time, I

would be the Booker with her name in
lights. The glory would go to me, not Ty,
Ro, or Marcellus, my three older brothers
who are good at everything.

3
I Didn't Plan for This

We all look forward to dinner on Thursday nights. That's when Ma whips up my favorite, most delicious dish, chicken enchiladas. I love those things! To make them just right, Ma leaves early from her dance studio

on Forty-seventh and Evers, where she gives daily lessons.

We kids were all sitting around the table waiting for the food when Ty stood up and pushed his chair in. "Excuse me, everybody," he said, "but I have a very important piece of news to share." Just then, Ro grabbed three black olives from the little bowl Ma keeps them in on the table. One by one, Ro *boinked* Ty in the head with the olives.

Ro said, "I've got a piece of news, too. You need to sit down, man. Nobody cares right now. I'm starvin' like Marvin!" Ro crunched a handful of tortilla chips into his mouth.

Marcellus said, "Come on, Ro, chill. Let Noodles say what he has to say." Marcellus called Ty by his nickname, Noodles. Then he popped a chip in his mouth, too.

Ma and Daddy came into the dining room, carrying the food and glasses of iced tea. Daddy usually misses Thursday's chicken enchiladas because he's working late at his music store, The Booker Box. I love The Booker Box. That's how I learned how to sing so well. My daddy has been bringing home all sorts of music since I was a baby.

Daddy must have heard us while he was in the kitchen. He set the food

on the table and then said, "Tyner
has some news? Share it with us,
little dude."

Ma and Daddy stood by Tyner. "Yeah,
baby, what is it?"

"Well, today at school, a lady
from the zoo brought a couple of

orangutans for us to see. But the real news is that she announced the big annual animal trivia contest for the whole school." Ty paused. "Well, the contest is really only for fifth-graders and up." Ty looked over at me. "Sorry, Rube. I know how good you are at trivia. But don't worry. I'll win this thing for you. I'm going to be representing the entire sixth grade." I wasn't expecting that at all. Ty was going to be in the contest?

Ma hugged Ty tight. "That's my baby! Congratulations, Tyner. I know you'll do well," Ma said. I didn't even tell them that I was going to try to be in the contest.

Daddy set down the plates in the center of the table so that we could each get our own chicken enchiladas. Ro beat us all. Before anyone could serve themselves, Ro's plate was spilling over with food. Ma flicked Ro on the hand with her pointer finger. "Don't be so greedy, boy!"

Then Marcellus stood up. He had an even bigger announcement. Something else I wasn't expecting, either.

"Not so fast, little brother. Somebody has to represent the seventh grade, right? I was chosen to be that guy," Marcellus said. Marcellus gave Ty the handshake that the Booker men do. We call it a pound of Booker. "May the best Booker win."

I slumped down in my chair. Usually when there was big news from anyone in our family, I clapped and shouted like it was *my* big news. But this time, my chin was hanging in my salsa. My eyes were full of tears, and I didn't even take a whiff of my enchilada. Ma came over from her chair and put her soft hands on my face. "It's okay, Ruby. You'll get your chance someday."

"Yeah, ladybug," Marcellus said. "One thing is for sure. A Booker *will* win this thing." Marcellus looked at his reflection in his spoon and gave us all a pretty-boy smile.

Ro just kept chomping his food. "Slow down, Roosevelt," Daddy joked. "You're going to bust a gut." Everybody but me filled their plates and bellies with Ma's enchiladas. I just couldn't eat. I kept thinking about what Marcellus said — that a Booker would win the contest. I wanted that Booker to be *me*. But with Ty and Marcellus in the competition, I worried that Booker would *not* be me.

4
Trivia Queen

The next day Miss Fuqua and I walked to the principal's office. Miss Fuqua was behind me 100 percent. She knew how much I wanted to be in the animal trivia contest.

"Okay, Ruby, cross your fingers. Let's hope Ms. Cherrybaum will allow you to enter the contest," Miss Fuqua said. "Do you think you can compete with the big kids? Are you ready to represent the third grade in front of the entire school?"

I stopped right before we were about to knock on Ms. Cherrybaum's office door. "Miss Fuqua, two of my big brothers will be in this contest, and they're older than me, but you know what? I don't care. I'm just going to try my best."

"Sounds like you're ready, Ruby Booker." Miss Fuqua smiled at me. She knocked on the glass door to the principal's office.

Ms. Cherrybaum greeted us at the door and called out, "Come in, come in, Miss Fuqua. How can I help you?" Sometimes Ms. Cherrybaum wears a pretty flower in her hair. But today she was wearing pearls and a bracelet. She

stood before us tall and pretty, with her hands on her hips. She looked down at me and said, "And how are you, Miss Ruby?"

"Fine, Ms. Cherrybaum. I'm doing just fine."

Miss Fuqua and I sat down in the chairs in front of the principal's desk. Ms. Cherrybaum sat on her desk. She crossed her legs, very ladylike, just like Ma teaches me to do. I crossed my legs, too. Miss Fuqua spoke up first.

"Well, Ms. Cherrybaum, we had an excellent visit by the Bellow Rock City head zookeeper yesterday, Coach Tuma's wife. Mrs. Tuma announced the big animal trivia contest and the prize, passes to the zoo. As you can imagine, my classroom was very excited about it."

"I see," Ms. Cherrybaum said. She crossed her legs in the other direction.

"But my students were disappointed that they won't be able to participate in the contest just because they're in the third grade." Miss Fuqua glanced at me. "One of my students wants to represent the third grade, and I feel she'd do an awesome job." Miss Fuqua believed in me so much.

"You have a third-grader who would like to compete?" Ms. Cherrybaum had her eyes on me. "Who is it?" Now I crossed my legs in the other direction.

"You're looking at her," I said, working hard not to blurt my answer. Miss Fuqua could see how serious I was about the contest. I didn't blink when I spoke. I looked straight up at Ms. Cherrybaum. Ms. Cherrybaum let me speak my mind. I liked that. "I can win those zoo passes," I said simply.

Ms. Cherrybaum talked real slow and gentle, like she was about to deliver bad news. "Miss Fuqua, remember last year? We allowed kids from all grade levels to compete in the trivia contest. There were second-

and third-graders who cried and threw tantrums when they lost. We don't want that again, since this year the contest will be on television," Ms. Cherrybaum explained.

My eyes turned into sparkling stars when she reminded us of the contest being on *television*. Ruby Marigold Booker — on TV! There was no way I was going to leave her office without being allowed to compete.

"Ms. Cherrybaum," I pleaded, "I am the trivia queen. My daddy brought a trivia book home as soon as I learned how to read. Ever since then, I've been reading trivia books, collecting trivia games, and playing cards. It's been about three years now," I said to the principal. "Don't believe I'm that good? Go ahead, throw out a category." Miss Fuqua looked at me like she wanted to say, "Are you sure?"

I was sure.

Ms. Cherrybaum curled her lips and raised her left eyebrow, thinking of something to ask me. Suddenly, she snapped her fingers and said, "Movies and plants. If you can tell me something about plants and the history of movies, you're in, Ruby."

"Let's see. Did you know that the first movie theater to ever open up was in Pittsburgh, Pennsylvania, in 1905? I just read about this. It was called the Nickelodeon." I folded my arms like my brother Ro does when he thinks he's done something cool.

"I *didn't* know that." Ms. Cherrybaum grinned. "Very impressive." Miss Fuqua smiled, too. "And what about plants? Got a good plant trivia fact?"

I did. I knew she would love this one. "Well, Ms. Cherrybaum, the largest flower in the world is in Indonesia. It can grow to be three feet across . . . I think . . . and weigh up to fifteen pounds! Isn't that something? You'd have a hard time putting that flower in your hair, huh, Ms. Cherrybaum!"

Miss Fuqua and Ms. Cherrybaum started cracking up. Ms. Cherrybaum got up, strolled to the back of her desk, and sat down in her seat. She took a deep breath. She looked me right in the eye and said, "Ruby, as long as you can promise me that you won't have a temper tantrum when those big kids answer tougher questions than you do, you're in. Represent your classroom and your grade level with pride."

"Thank you, thank you, thank you, Ms. Cherrybaum!!!" I jumped into Miss Fuqua's arms and gave her a hug that probably surprised her. She hugged me back. I was so happy to have this chance, I busted out singing in Ms. Cherrybaum's office. I couldn't help it.

"I'm in! I'm in!
I know that I can win.
I'm in! I'm in!"

But I knew it wasn't going to be easy, especially with Ty and Marcellus representing their grade levels.

Miss Fuqua walked me to the music room so that I could join up with the rest of the kids from Pluto-3. When I walked in, they were singing a song about a tadpole with the hiccups. I'd never heard that song before. But when they all saw me, it got really quiet. They were waiting to hear if I was allowed to be in the contest. I walked to the choir stand, where my classmates were lined up. My head was hung low like I was super-duper sad. Then, all of a sudden, I jumped up with my hands reaching toward the ceiling and yelled, "I'M IN! I'M IN!"

The music room turned into a party. Even our music teacher, Mr. Dilla, jumped up and down and celebrated with us. I don't think he knew what we were happy about, but Mr. Dilla is just that type of teacher. He gets happy when we get happy.

I couldn't wait to tell my brothers. The trivia queen was now in the contest. And I didn't get in it to lose.

❀ ★ ❀ ★ 5 ❀ ★ ❀ ★
I'll Do It My Way

I always meet my brothers by the front gates of the school grounds. I couldn't wait to tell them the good news. But when I got there, I only saw Ro, standing alone.

"Hey, Ruby. What took you so long?" Ro asked before he scooped a handful of worms from a muddy puddle and pretended to come after two girls who passed by him. The girls took off screaming and ran onto their bus. Ro threw the worms back down. He knew I wasn't afraid of worms.

"I have some good news. Where are Ty and Marcellus?" I asked Ro.

"Ty and Marcellus? They had something very *important* to do. It's just you and me, shorty," Ro replied.

"Important?" I said. "The good news I have is super-extra-big important. I'm going to —" I was about to tell Ro my news when he cut me off.

"You're going to be in the big, goofy, animal trivia thing. I know," Ro said with a smirk on his face. I couldn't believe he knew.

"How did you —" I tried to say before he cut me off again. Ro can be so rude.

"Nothing gets past me, Ruby. There's a kid in your class who has a sister in my class. Good news travels fast, baby sis." Ro grinned as he patted himself on the back.

"So, do Ty and Marcellus know about me being in the animal trivia contest?" I asked Ro.

"Do they know? Girl, the reason they're not here is because they're getting ready for the contest. They're off studying animal facts."

"What!?! We've gotta get going,

then." I grabbed Ro by the arm and took off, running down Hope Road.

"Wait a minute. Slow down! Slow down!" Ro put the brakes on me. "You don't have to worry about Ty or Marcellus. I can help."

Ro? Helping me? I sure wanted to know how. "What do *you* plan to do?"

"If I help you, it'll be the Ro Rowdy way," he said, calling himself by his nickname. Before I knew it, we turned the corner onto Fifty-fifth Street.

Ro bought a hot dog from one of the snack cart guys on the corner. He knows Ma hates it when we eat junk before we get home, but sometimes he does it anyway.

"And what's the Ro Rowdy way? Cheating?" I asked, knowing the answer was going to be yes.

We sat down on a bench outside of Big Man's Laundromat and Biscuits. "It's not really cheating, it's . . . getting even," Ro said. "I was twelve votes short of representing the sixth grade in this animal trivia thing. Twelve!"

"Did you really think you were going to be picked over Ty?" I asked. If I were in the sixth grade, I would have voted for Ty, too.

"At least I had a chance. Besides, I've got brains, too, Ruby." Ro defended his smartness. Even though he gets the lowest grades of all four of us, his grades are still good. That is, when he's not in some kind of trouble.

I watched Ro take the last bite of his hot dog. Even though he wasn't supposed to be eating it, it sure did look good. "So what's your problem with Marcellus? Why would you help me beat him?" I asked.

"Are you kidding me? Can you imagine the look on Mr. Big-Time's face when he's just been beaten by his baby sis? That would be classic,"

Ro said, calling Marcellus by his nickname.

As we continued down Fifty-fifth Street and then turned onto our street, Chill Brook Avenue, Ro shared his plans to help me beat Ty and Marcellus. "Ty will read all of his science books, or he's going to use the Internet to learn about every single animal on the planet." Ro began to draw out plans like he was a coach.

"So what are you saying we should do?" I asked.

"Well, since Ty and I are roommates, I could jack up the computer in our room so that he'll have a hard time finding anything on animals. Marcellus will be using his own computer, you'll have your laptop, and you know Ma and Daddy don't like us on theirs."

"What about all his books?"

"Ruby, don't you know that I'm a magician, too? I can make those books vanish, my dear." Ro rubbed his chin like he had a beard. He laughed like a villain.

"Magician? Jacking up the computer? I don't even want to know what you've got planned for Marcellus. Besides, *I am not a cheater, Ro!*" I said, making sure he heard me loud and clear.

* * *

As we got closer and closer to our brownstone, it seemed like everyone we passed said hello.

"Hey, Roosevelt."

"Nice book bag, Ruby. Is that a real guitar?"

"Staying out of trouble, Ro?"

At least six people asked Ro if he was staying out of trouble. Of course, he wasn't. He was trying to get me mixed up in his crazy plans.

"I'm not helping you, Ro," I said.

"Suit yourself, shorty." Ro shrugged his shoulders and started to walk up our steps. He looked back at me and chuckled. "You're good at trivia and everything, but do you really think you have a chance to win against Noodles and Big-Time? The brains, and the kid who wins everything? I don't think so. Good luck."

Ro walked inside. I stood there on our stoop, watching the cars go by.

Later that night, when I told Ma and Daddy that I'd be competing in the trivia contest, they both hugged me at the same time. Ma said, "Ruby, you're representing the third grade *and* the Booker women. I know you'll make everyone proud."

"Ruby, I know you'll do the Bookers proud. No matter what, you're already a trivia queen," Daddy said. Even though Daddy was right, I started to wonder what I had gotten myself into.

6
Getting Ready, Getting Scared

On Saturday morning, I woke up before the sun. I washed my face and put on something cute (of course). I picked up Lady Love, my pet iguana, and slid with her down the stair rail to meet everybody for breakfast. When I got to the kitchen, the boys were already gone. Ma and Daddy were at the table, eating oatmeal and toast and staring into each other's eyes, all lovey-dovey.

"Excuse me, guys." I giggled.

"Where are the boys?" I asked. Ma wiped Daddy's mouth with a napkin.

"Ty is across the street using his friend Macklin's computer. His and Roosevelt's computer got some kind of flu," Daddy explained.

Ma stroked the top of Lady Love's head. "Roosevelt is down at Freedom Park skateboarding with his buddies," she said.

Daddy kissed me and Ma on the cheek. "Marcellus is on his way down to The Booker Box. There's a DVD and a CD-ROM about animals he wants. I'm going there now," Daddy said. Then he walked out the door to meet Marcellus.

Ma filled a bowl of oatmeal for me. "So where are you headed today, Ruby? Did you have anything planned with the boys?" she asked me.

"No, Ma. You know I'm in the animal trivia contest this Tuesday. Trivia is so easy for me, but Ma, how am I going to compete against Ty and Marcellus?" I sat down next to Ma and put my head in her lap.

"Now, I know this is not *my* Ruby Marigold Booker talking. Let me see your face. I need to make sure it's really you." Ma lifted my head and looked in my eyes. "Yeah, it's you. Haven't you started to prepare for the contest?" she asked.

"That's why I got up so early today," I explained. "But I guess it wasn't early enough. The boys are already getting ready. I was headed to the library, but I might be too late."

"It's never too late, Ruby. You're still early, but why are you going to the library? You know so much already, and you have a ton of trivia books, cards, and games right here. Besides, you've been preparing for this ever since Daddy bought you your first trivia book, before you were in the first grade."

"I know. But maybe there's something I still don't know. Since Ty and Marcellus are older than me, they just know more stuff." I was talking really fast. I do that when I get nervous.

"Baby, everything you need is upstairs in your room and upstairs in that fabulous, colorful, wild and crazy brain of yours," Ma said. Ma's words really helped me not be so scared. "If you need me to help you study anything, I'll sit with you after we come back from the studio."

"Ma, I can't go to the dance studio with you. I need to start going over my trivia stuff *now*," I said.

"Ruby, it'll be fine. Go upstairs and put Lady Love back in her aquarium. Grab a book, those trivia cards on animals, and let's go," Ma said.

"Ma, I won't be able to study *and* dance."

"I'm not asking you to dance, baby. I have two classes to teach, but I will help you go over anything you might need to cover for the contest." Ma kissed me on the top of my head.

"Ma, are you going to help Ty and Marcellus, too?" I asked. I wondered who she was cheering for the most. "I mean, do you think they're going to beat me?"

"I think that I have a group of brilliant children. I won't be surprised by whoever wins, because you're all winners to me. Now, go upstairs and get your things, Ms. Trivia Queen."

I'm the queen of trivia and Ma is the queen of saying things to make everybody feel good.

* * *

In between showing her dance students how to do new steps, Ma spun over to me, grabbed a trivia card, and asked me a question or two.

"The moose is the state animal for which state?"

"Uhh . . . Maine!"

"Correct!"

This went on all morning. Ma asked me a question, then twirled back to her dance students. Ma can sure do a lot of stuff at once. Sometimes it seems like magic, but I guess it's just something mothers know how to do.

We walked home after Ma's dance classes. All of the boys had come back home, too. Ro was in his room playing some new baseball video game. I tiptoed down the hall to peek into Marcellus's room. He was lying on his bed watching the DVD on animals. Marcellus's study habits are weird, but they work for him.

I leaned into Ty's room quietly. He didn't see me, either. He was reading a whole stack of science books.

I felt like I was on a roller coaster. When I was with Ma, it seemed like maybe I could win this thing. But when I saw Ty and Marcellus getting

ready for the contest, it showed me that they meant business. I started to worry again. In three days we'd find out if I really was a winner.

I went to my room and spread my trivia cards all over my bed. Lady

Love chomped on banana chips while I studied the cards. Between trivia facts, I kept saying to myself, *Let no Booker boy stand in your way of making history. . . .*

Lady Love fell asleep. Before I knew it, I was starting to doze off, too. I fell asleep saying to myself, *Let no Booker . . . boy stand in . . . your way of making . . . history. . . .*

The funny thing was, the more I said it, the less I was able to convince myself.

7

Believe in What You Got

I woke up to somebody banging on my bedroom door.

My trivia cards were all over the place. They covered up the purple-and-orange piano keys rug on my floor. "Who is it!?" I hollered.

"It's me, baby. It's your daddy."

I got up and ran over to the door to let Daddy in. When I opened the door, he greeted me with his big old smile. He had a hand behind his back. He was hiding something.

I folded my arms, rolled my eyes at him, and said, "Daddy, are you trying to surprise me? What's behind your back?"

He laughed. "I just can't pull anything over on you, huh, cutie-pie?"

"Nope," I said with my arms still folded.

"Well, I thought I'd bring you something to feed your brain and to help you prepare for your TV trivia contest." From behind his back, he pulled out a big bowl of my favorite ice cream, peanut butter and jelly. There's only one place in Bellow Rock City that sells PB&J ice cream, and it's across town. Daddy gets it for me anyway. He's so cool.

"Thank you so much, Daddy!" I hugged him and kissed him on the cheek. "I really could use this. Peanut butter and jelly ice cream *is* good for the brain."

Daddy took a seat at my desk. "So, how is everything coming? I mean, are you ready for the big time?"

"I don't know, Daddy. It felt like I was ready when I was doing trivia cards with Ma this morning at her dance studio, but now I'm not too sure."

"Ruby Booker, the one who gave

herself the title Trivia Queen, is afraid of a little trivia contest?" Daddy had a surprised look on his face.

"Daddy, I *know* I'm a trivia queen, but what if all this getting ready is still not enough?"

"Come on now, Ruby. Don't be so down on yourself. You're the best trivia mind I know. And I'm not just saying that because you're my daughter."

"Really, Daddy?"

"Sure, Ruby. Nobody sings as well as you do, and nobody knows strange and crazy facts like you do. You have to believe in the things that you do well," Daddy said.

"You're right, Daddy. I don't know why I'm stressing," I said. It seemed like a little light went off in my head. "But . . . just to make sure . . . would you mind?"

I handed Daddy a stack of my trivia cards.

"No problem, sweetheart. You know I'd help you anytime," Daddy said with that big smile.

Daddy shuffled the cards and was about to ask me a bunch of questions about sea animals when we heard four knocks at the door. It was Ro. I know his knocks. He always does four.

"Can we help you?" I asked, because I knew he just wanted to start some trouble.

"The question is . . . can I help y*ou?*" Ro said. And then he really shocked me and Daddy. He held out his hand for the cards and then asked, "Daddy, would you mind if I went over some questions with Ruby? I mean, I'll probably go a little faster than you, especially with you being old and stuff," Ro joked. Daddy picked Ro up and spun him around like a helicopter, then tossed him on the bed.

"Can an old man do *that,*

Roosevelt?" Daddy said. Ro bounced on my bed and laughed like crazy. I wasn't laughing, though. Daddy knows I don't like it when my bed gets rumpled.

Daddy handed the cards to Ro. "Ruby, is that okay with you? Would you mind if Roosevelt took my place?"

I crossed my arms, looked Ro up and down, and wondered what he was really up to. "I guess so. But don't waste my time, boy," I said, and I meant it.

"I won't waste your time. Promise," Ro said.

Daddy left, and Ro bounced off my bed and onto the floor. He began to ask me questions from the cards right away. "The most dolphins are found in what ocean?"

"Wait! Wait! Wait!" I yelled. "One minute you want to help me by cheating, and the next minute you bust in here and want to help me the right way. Are you feeling okay, Ro?" I asked as I put a hand on his forehead to check his temperature.

"Ruby, I was just thinking, I don't want you to go into this contest and not give Ty Noodles, Big-Time Marcellus, and the rest of those kids a good match. If helping you go over a few questions is all it's going to take, I can stomach it."

"Well, what happened to doing it the *Ro* way?" I asked.

"Most of the time, doing things my way works. But I realized that the Ro way is not the *Ruby* way of doing things," Ro explained. "All four of us do things differently, but what works for me might not work for you. What works for Ty might not work for Marcellus. And even though I mess with you sometimes, I still — I mean, you are my sister and everything," Ro mumbled. This was the first time I had ever seen him try to *really, really, really* help me.

"Cool beans. Thank you, Ro," I said.

I reached out to grab Ro's hand with the cards in it. He let me hold his hand for a few seconds. That was my way of showing Ro how happy I was that he was helping me — the right way.

Then Ro pulled his hand away and said, "Girl, do you want me to help you, or do you want to play patty-cake? The contest is three days away. Let's do this."

"Okay, okay. I'm ready." I winked at Ro. "Let's do this."

❀⋆❀⋆★ 8 ❀⋆❀⋆★
Get Your Game Face On

"**M**aaaaaa! *Come on!* I'm not even *in* this stupid animal trivia thing. Why do I have to look nice?" Ro cried. Ma was buttoning up a starched white shirt for Ro and putting one of Daddy's blue-and-white-striped ties on him. He actually looked good.

Ma said, "Boy, stay still while I fork out these wild curls of yours. Doesn't your brother look nice, Tyner? Marcellus?" Ma asked the other boys.

"Yes, Ma," Ty and Marcellus said like zombies as they pulled at their ties and jackets. Ty likes wearing bow ties. Marcellus is big enough to wear some of Daddy's nice clothes now. To tell you the truth, they all looked nice — but not as together as I did.

When I came in the room, I stole the show. Daddy introduced me like I was a TV star. "Ladies and gentlemen, introducing the third-grade representative in this year's animal trivia contest, the one, the only . . . Miss Ruby Booker!!!"

I twirled into the room in a nice

jean jumper Ma had made, a pretty angel-white shirt, white bracelets on both wrists, and a pair of cute white jingly earrings. The earrings were clip-ons, but that was okay with me. Plus, my jumper had fancy orange paw prints on it. I couldn't stop looking at myself in the mirror.

We went downstairs and had a quick breakfast. Tyner read over a few animal-fact cards. Ro kept pulling at his necktie. Marcellus popped hard-boiled eggs into his mouth like they were marshmallows.

"Son, if you don't stop, you'll regret it later on today," Daddy told Marcellus. After about five eggs, Marcellus gulped a glass of buttermilk, then we all piled into Daddy's van. Ma didn't want us to walk. She knows how fast we get dirty.

Ma and Daddy dropped us off at school. "We'll be up as soon as the contest begins," Daddy said. Ma blew us all a kiss.

Before Daddy drove off, Ma called out to Ro and said, "Baby, keep that tie on *all* day. You look so handsome. Doesn't he, Ruby?" she asked.

"He sure does, Ma," I agreed. Then we walked into school and hurried to our classrooms.

When I opened the door of Pluto-3, everybody jumped up and screamed,

"GO GET 'EM, RUBY! WIN US THOSE FREE PASSES!" And it wasn't just my classmates. Mr. Littlejohn's third-grade class was there, too.

"Go get 'em, Ruby. Win it for the third grade!" cheered Lenny, one of the boys I clobbered at ball tag.

"Yeah, Ruby, if you can beat us, I know you'll do great in this contest," said Mikey, the other boy I beat from Mr. Littlejohn's class.

"Thanks, guys," I answered.

Miss Fuqua had the room decorated with banners, signs, and balloons. "We are so proud of you, Ruby Booker," she said.

"This is so nice, guys." I clutched my guitar book bag like a teddy bear. Everything was so nice. Everyone was looking at me, even Miss Fuqua and Mr. Littlejohn, like they were waiting for me to say something important.

"Well . . . I'll do my best for everyone in the third grade. You, too, Miss Fuqua and Mr. Littlejohn." They broke out into cheers and clapped again. All of that attention made me feel good, but now I felt more pressure to win.

The office secretary, Miss Funkhouser, came around to the classrooms to pick up the five kids who were in the contest: me for the

third grade, a fifth-grade girl named
Sunshine Winfrey, of course Ty for
the sixth grade, Marcellus for the
seventh, and an eighth-grade boy
everybody calls J.W.

Miss Funkhouser took us to the
auditorium before any of the other
students were there. The TV crew

was hooking up cameras and microphones. We were seated in the front row, and the stage looked really big to me. There were five microphones already placed on the stage. Just by looking at them, I could tell that the shortest one was mine.

Ty was on one side of me, and he still looked nice. Marcellus was on the other side of me. His clothes were still neat, but his face had a weird expression on it.

"Are you okay, Marcellus?" I asked as I grabbed his hand. His other hand was over his tummy.

"It's just a little . . . rumbling in my

belly. I'm cool," he said. But I could tell something was bothering him. Maybe he was as nervous as I was, or more.

Ty was ready, though. He stared straight ahead at the stage and didn't speak to anyone. He was serious.

Soon the auditorium started to fill up with kids, teachers, and parents. Each grade level sat in their own part of the auditorium and carried signs to cheer on the person representing them. Everyone wanted to win those free year-round passes to the Bellow Rock City Zoo.

When we got onstage and stood in front of our microphones, I saw a big board that stood to the side. It had the titles of every category in the contest. That's when a gigantic bullfrog got stuck in my throat, and my head felt like a ball on a Ping-Pong table. And for a second, my tummy started to rock back and forth like a little boat lost in the ocean. There were a few things on that board that I just didn't know too much about:

Kangaroo life
Snake facts

Birds, birds, birds
Types of tigers
The truth about rhinos

There were at least ten of those titles that I was clueless about. Maybe I knew some stuff, but just a little. I took a lot of deep breaths. Ty noticed my heavy breathing. He finally said to me, "Rube, don't look so worried. You're going to do great. It looks like we have some easy questions coming our way." He smiled.

Easy questions? Those titles on the board didn't look easy to me.

I took a big gulp and then looked out into the audience and saw Ma and Daddy! Ma had her camera. She was taking pictures before anything even started. I could hear her saying, "Those are my babies. One. Two. Three. I've got three of my babies up there. Hey, Ruby, Tyner, Marcellus!"

Mrs. Tuma from the zoo walked out onto the stage and welcomed everyone in the audience. "I'll be the one asking the questions," she said. "Are you ready to begin?"

The TV cameras were on us, the microphones were on, and so were we.

The wait was over. And just like

that, the annual Hope Road Academy
animal trivia contest began.

One of the five contestants was
going to win, and win big.

✿★✿★ 9 ✿★✿★
The Showdown

The eighth-grader, J.W., was the first one up.

Mrs. Tuma began the questions. "The Bengal tiger is from which country?"

I knew this one! The answer was India. But it wasn't my turn so I had to keep quiet.

J.W. answered slowly. "China?"

"I'm sorry, J.W.," Mrs. Tuma said. "That's not correct."

J.W. threw his head back.

"The correct answer is India," Mrs. Tuma said.

J.W. shook his head as he left the stage. I heard him say quietly, "I *knew* it was India."

The eighth-graders in the audience booed him. So J.W. was

gone. It was sad how his classmates booed him, but the contest kept rolling.

Next up was the fifth-grade girl, Sunshine Winfrey.

Mrs. Tuma asked, "Which continent is the only one on the planet that doesn't have snakes?"

Mrs. Tuma gave Sunshine three choices: a) Africa, b) Asia, and c) Antarctica.

"Asia," Sunshine answered, all proud, like she was certain. I don't know what books Sunshine had been reading, but the only continent without snakes is Antarctica. I knew that answer two years ago. So Sunshine Winfrey was gone.

The only ones left in the contest were us Bookers. Ma was going bonkers. She snatched a sign from one of my classmates and held up another with Ty's and Marcellus's names on it.

"THOSE ARE MY BABIES! ZOOM IN, CAMERAMAN. ZOOM IN!" Ma yelled. She was so proud.

"We're down to three contestants. Am I correct in understanding that you three are related?" Mrs. Tuma asked.

Ty was our unofficial spokes-Booker. "Yes, ma'am, we are." Ty looked over at me. "This is my baby sis, Ruby." Then he looked at Marcellus. "And that's my older brother, Marcellus."

"Hi, everybody." Marcellus moaned, holding his queasy tummy. The seventh-graders hollered and screamed.

"Marcellus! Marcellus!" Some called him by his nickname, "Go, Big-Time!"

It was my turn to say hello to the crowd. I stepped up to the microphone. As soon as I opened my mouth, my mic let out a loud screeching noise. It sounded like an angry witch. Everyone covered their

ears. The screech stopped, but then my microphone didn't work. I spoke into it, but no one could hear me. "Hello? Mic check — one, two, one, three." I couldn't answer any questions. Mrs. Tuma looked at me and shrugged her shoulders. There was nothing she could do.

All of a sudden, Marcellus shoved his microphone toward me and said, "Here, ladybug, you can have mine." He turned completely green, put both hands over his mouth, and then ran off the stage, down the main aisle of the auditorium, and out the door. Daddy jumped up and ran after him. I knew those eggs were not going to treat him so well. Poor Marcellus. I guess the good thing for him was that he didn't really lose the contest. It was his stomach that lost its breakfast!

It was down to Ty and me. I was beginning to worry about my chances of winning. Mrs. Tuma started with Ty. "Mr. Booker, true or false? Tarantulas spin big webs."

Ty snapped his fingers. "That's a piece of cake, Mrs. Tuma. The answer is false. Tarantulas do not spin webs."

"That's correct, Mr. Booker. That entitles you to another question."

The other sixth-graders clapped and clapped for Ty. Ty licked his lips. He was so ready for the next question.

Mrs. Tuma asked, "What's the name of a baby kangaroo?"

I knew this one, too! I mouthed the answer as Ty said it into the microphone. "A joey."

Mrs. Tuma paused. She looked out over the audience. Everyone waited . . .

"Right," Mrs. Tuma said. "A baby kangaroo is called a joey."

Big cheers for Ty. Even I wanted to cheer for him. But according to the rules, it was my turn now, even though Ty had answered two questions in a row.

Mrs. Tuma turned to me. I wiped my sweaty hands on my jumper. Mrs. Tuma pulled out a question card.

"Ruby, what kind of bird is a cockatoo: a) parrot, b) type of pigeon, or c) a member of the goose family?"

I shook my hands free of their sweat. This was one of the facts I'd learned from Daddy. Ty's eyes never left me.

"A cockatoo is a kind of parrot," I said.

Mrs. Tuma smiled. "That's correct, Ruby."

I did a little dance. I *knew* I was right. Now it was the third-graders cheering loudest. Even that quiet kid, Low-Low, was cheering.

"Next question," Mrs. Tuma said. Everyone settled down. "How does a whale breathe?"

First *I* had to remember to breathe. Then I answered. "Through a blowhole at the top of its head."

"Correct, Ruby," Mrs. Tuma said.

"Yes!" I stomped my foot. The whole auditorium was cheering now. The heat was on big-time.

Mrs. Tuma cleared her throat and said, "Now that you've both answered two questions correctly, we will go back and forth with the questions. We have a good match going on at Hope Road Academy." That's when the auditorium cheered way loud. Mrs. Tuma explained, "At this point in the contest, the format changes a little. If you answer a question incorrectly, you won't be out unless your opponent answers the next question correctly." Then Mrs. Tuma grabbed another question card and asked me, "Rhinos are in the same family as: a) elephants, b) seals, or c) horses?"

I eased up to the microphone but paused. Suddenly, my brain went blank. I looked out toward my classmates, but they couldn't help me. I had no idea what the answer was. Finally, I opened my mouth and said, "Is it . . . elephants?"

Mrs. Tuma looked at Ty, looked at me, looked out into the audience, and then said, "I'm sorry, Ruby." My shoulders slumped and my classmates moaned. I felt like it was all over. But in order for Ty to win, he had to answer the next question correctly.

"Okay, sixth-grade rep, if you answer this one, you will win free year-round passes to the Bellow Rock City Zoo for everyone in the sixth grade." She asked Ty, "Would you like to answer that question or a new one?"

For some reason he said, "I'll take a new one."

I was still onstage, because if Ty got the next question wrong, I would have another turn.

"I'm ready, Mrs. Tuma," Ty said politely.

"How many minutes can a green iguana stay underwater: a) ten minutes, b) an hour, or c) twenty-eight minutes?"

And for the first time ever, Ty froze. It looked like his brain had hit a wall. "Umm . . . ummm," he looked trapped. "Ummmm . . . ten minutes?" He said it like he wasn't really sure. It seemed like he didn't really think about his answer.

Mrs. Tuma looked at me. She turned her eyes to Ty, then for a long minute watched the audience. "I'm sorry, Ty, that's not correct," she finally said.

When she said that, my eyes lit up like I was a lamp and somebody flipped on the switch. Iguanas are my favorite subject. Because of Lady Love, I know everything about them. Before it was too late, I held my hand up and asked Mrs. Tuma, "Would it be okay if I answered that question?"

Mrs. Tuma glanced at the trivia card again. "Sure," she said. I had to keep from jumping up and down! "I'll read the question again. How many minutes can a green iguana stay underwater?"

Before I could answer, I heard Ma say, "You got it, baby! I know you can answer this one!" And you know what? She was right. Before I answered, I thought about what Ma had told me on Saturday. She said that everything I needed to win was already in my head — and she was right!

"Mrs. Tuma . . . I believe the correct answer is," I eased up to the microphone and paused for just a second. "C. Twenty-eight minutes."

Mrs. Tuma looked at the correct answer on the back of her card and then said, "Ladies and gentlemen, the winner of the Hope Road Academy animal trivia contest, and the recipient of free Bellow Rock City Zoo passes for a year, is the third grade!" My section, the two third-grade classes, went crazy. Even Miss Fuqua and Mr. Littlejohn gave each other a high five.

Ty looked over to me and said, "Congratulations, Rube. I knew you could do it." And you know what? He was right.

Ms. Cherrybaum came out and gave me a big trophy, a ribbon, and an envelope filled with free passes to the zoo for all of the third-graders. "Congrats, Miss Booker. You've made Hope Road Academy very proud," she said. I represented my class, my grade, and my family the best way I knew how — Ruby-style.

Before we walked off the stage, I scooted up to my microphone and answered the question that I'd missed earlier. It just came to me. "By the way . . . rhinos are related to horses.

Just thought you guys would like to know that. Thank you."

Man, that felt good!

✿★✿★ 10 ✿★✿★
Spread the Love

On Saturday, Daddy made a date to use our free Bellow Rock City Zoo passes. It was a beautiful day and a perfect day to see a bunch of animals and to eat cotton candy and peanuts. When Daddy and I came outside, Ty, Ro, and Marcellus were on the stoop. They didn't look too happy.

"Have a good time, ladybug," Marcellus mumbled as he tapped a set of drumsticks on the steps.

"Yeah, Rube, have fun at the zoo. Take some pictures for me," Ty added, while leaning over Ro's shoulder to watch Ro play his portable video game.

"Whatever, Ruby," Ro said. "Daddy, bring back a candy apple for me, will ya?" Ro didn't even look up once to congratulate me.

"Thanks for telling me how good a job I did on Tuesday, Ro," I said. I playfully pushed him in the head when I walked past.

When Daddy and I got to the bottom of the steps, I turned around, faced the boys, and said, "Come on, guys, did you think I would leave you hanging like that? Especially you, Ro. You were so helpful getting me ready for the contest. I couldn't forget to thank my big bro Ro. And I sure couldn't forget to celebrate the other Booker boys for going up against the trivia queen supreme."

"What are you talking about?" Marcellus asked. They all looked puzzled.

"Well, you know that everyone in the third grade won free passes to the zoo, right?" I asked my brothers.

They all spoke at the same time, "Right."

"Seeing how I was the big winner . . . they also gave me enough free passes for my whooooole family. Who's the girl? Who's the girl!?" I asked excitedly. They jumped down to the sidewalk where I stood and gave me a big group hug.

"She tricked you fellas, huh, guys?" Daddy asked the boys.

"Not me, Daddy. I knew that Ruby would come through." Ro chuckled.

"Yeah, right," Marcellus replied with a big smile. Ma came out wearing a bright yellow sundress. She looked pretty, as usual. She had the passes in her hand. Before she gave each boy his own pass, she asked them, "Okay, boys, so who do we have to thank for this wonderful gift?" She looked at me and winked.

Then they all came over to hug me again and said, "Thanks, Ruby!"

I laughed. Daddy laughed. We all laughed, hopped into the van, and then drove to the zoo, where we had the greatest time ever.

All hail Bellow Rock City's queen of trivia — Ruby Marigold Booker!

Well, just like my Daddy told me, "Ruby, you have to believe in the things you do well." And that's the truth. The thing is, everybody in the world has something they do best. I'm a real, true Trivia Queen. And now I've got the free zoo passes to prove it! —rb

☆ The Ruby Challenge ☆

Of course, there's only one Ruby Marigold Booker. But now that I've been crowned Trivia Queen Supreme, I'm ready to share my glory with anyone who can match my royal status.

Here's my very own animal quiz. Take the Ruby challenge, and see if you, too, could get free passes to the zoo.

Unlike the Hope Road Academy trivia contest, where only Mrs. Tuma knew the answers, my test has the answers at the end. No peeking allowed!

(If you answer all ten correctly, ask your parents to take you to the zoo.)

RUBY'S ROYAL SUPREME TRIVIA TEST

1. Which animal runs the fastest?
   a) Lion
   b) Cheetah
   c) Horse
   d) Grizzly bear
2. True or False: All zebras have stripes that are exactly alike.
3. Which animal is the world's largest mammal?
   a) Human
   b) Giraffe
   c) Shark
   d) Blue whale

4. Baby penguins are called:

   a) Chicks

   b) Ducklings

   c) Little penguins

   d) Babes

5. A female turkey is called a:

   a) Lady turkey

   b) Tom

   c) Hen

   d) Gizzard

6. True or false: Spiders do not have skeletons.

7. True or false: All spiders spin webs.

8. True or false: All spiders produce silk.

9. What is the name of a baby frog?

a) Slimy

b) Tadpole

c) Froggy

d) Bullfrog

10. What is the largest land animal?

a) Cheetah

b) Bear

c) African elephant

d) Lion

11. What's the difference between an herbivore and a carnivore?

12. True or false: The rhinoceros has a life span ranging from 25 to 45 years.

Answers

1: b) Cheetah **2:** False. No two zebras have stripes that are exactly alike. **3:** d) Blue whale **4:** a) Chicks **5:** c) Hen **6:** True. They have an outer shell called an exoskeleton. **7:** False **8:** True **9:** b) Tadpole **10:** c) African elephant **11:** Herbivores eat plants; carnivores eat meat. **12:** True

★ In the next Ruby book, ★ you're invited to Ruby Booker's super-splendid slumber party! But there's no time to sleep when Ruby and her crew set out to teach Ro a lesson he won't forget....

The last time Ruby had friends over for a slumber party, her older brother, Roosevelt, aka Ro, pranked and scared the girls all night long. Now it's payback time! Ruby and the girls make up their minds to teach Ro a valuable lesson, using all the tools at their disposal, including a little bit of lipstick and a lot of Ruby style. Bottom line — don't mess with Ruby Booker! Read *The Slumber Party Payback* to find out why.

✫ About the Author ✫

Derrick Barnes is the author of the series Ruby and the Booker Boys: *Brand-new School, Brave New Ruby* and *Trivia Queen, 3rd Grade Supreme.* He's also written *Stop, Drop, and Chill* and *Low-down Bad Day Blues* as well as books for young adults. He is a native of Kansas City, Missouri, although he spent a good portion of his formative years in Mississippi. A graduate of Jackson State University, he has written bestselling copy for various Hallmark Cards lines and was the first African-American male staff writer for Hallmark. Derrick and his wife, Tinka, reside in Kansas City with their own version of the Booker boys — Ezra, Solomon, and Silas.